P9-DMZ-027

THE DAVID HALE LIBRARY

11861

GOLD FEVER

VERLA KAY

ILLUSTRATIONS BY

S. D. SCHINDLER

DAVID HALE LIBRARY
MARIN PRIMARY SCHOOL
20 MAGNOLIA AVENUE
LARKSPUR, CA 94939

G. P. PUTNAM'S SONS · NEW YORK

AUTHOR'S NOTE

GOLD! Word got out in 1849 that this precious yellow metal had been found, and the fever that gripped the world was so intense that California became a bustling state just one year later. During the first five years of the Gold Rush, 150,000 people moved to California, and most of them were miners. They dug their way through the state, tossing up ramshackle mining towns wherever there were reports of a good find. Then, when the gold played out, the miners deserted the towns just as quickly, leaving hundreds of ghost towns behind.

The artwork was done in colored pencil on recycled flecked paper.

Text copyright © 1999 by Verla Kay Bradley. Illustrations copyright © 1999 by S. D. Schindler.   All rights reserved. This book, or parts thereof, may not be reproduced in any form without permission in writing from the publisher, G. P. Putnam's Sons, a division of Penguin Putnam Books for Young Readers, 345 Hudson Street, New York, NY 10014. G. P. Putnam's Sons, Reg. U.S. Pat. & Tm. Off. Published simultaneously in Canada. Printed in Hong Kong by South China Printing Co. (1988) Ltd. Book design by Gunta Alexander. Text set in Cheltenham.

Library of Congress Cataloging-in-Publication Data
Kay, Verla. Gold Fever / Verla Kay; illustrated by S. D. Schindler.   p.   cm.   Summary: In this brief rhyming story set during the gold rush, Jasper leaves his family and farm to pursue his dream of finding gold. [1. Gold mines and mining—Fiction. 2. West (U.S.)—Fiction. 3. Stories in rhyme.] I. Schindler, S. D., ill. II. Title. PZ8.3.K225Go 1999 [E]—dc21   97-49634 CIP AC   ISBN 0-399-23027-0   10 9 8 7 6 5 4 3 2 1   First Impression

For my loving and supportive husband, Terry,
whose grimy, grinning face greeted and
inspired me every time he returned home
from a gold-panning expedition —V. K.

Dashing westward,
Many miners.
Townsfolk snicker,
"Forty-niners."

Jasper sighing,
Dreaming dreams:
"GOLD! There's *gold*
In them thar streams."

Packed a shovel,
Pistol, pick,
Goldpan, bedroll,
Walking stick.

No more barnyard,
Pitchfork, hoe,
Farmhouse, family,
"Got to go."

Prairie—dust storm,
River, rocks.

Desert, sagebrush,

Holes in socks.

Vultures, bleached bones,
Craggy knoll.
Empty canteen,
Water hole!

Granite mountain,
Grizzly bear.
Rocky outcrop,
Bobcat's lair.

California,
Gold and green.
Crowded diggings,
Long tom, stream.

Icy water,
Wet feet, cold.
Sluicing, panning,
"Where's the gold?"

Grumpy miners,
Nuggets—*small*.
Jasper scowling,
Fireside brawl.

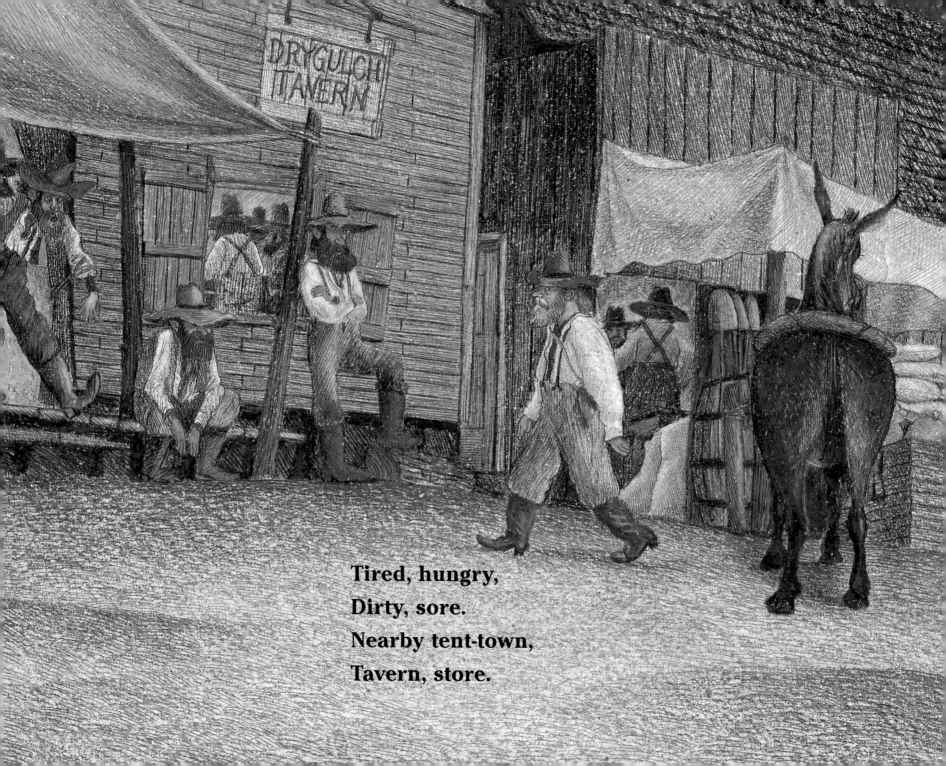

Tired, hungry,
Dirty, sore.
Nearby tent-town,
Tavern, store.

Coffee, bacon,
Sugar, beans.
Empty pockets,
Jasper's jeans.

Back to pry bar,
Heavy pails,
Rocker, cradle,
Hammer, nails.

Busting bedrock,
Boulder rolled.

Shovel, digging;

"Where's the gold?"

Narrow quartz vein,
Tiny flakes.
Rocky crevice,
"Rattlesnakes!"

Crusty long johns,
Smelly shirt.
Sweat-stained britches
Caked with dirt.

No gold pockets,
No rich vein.
Jasper leaving,
Quitting claim.

Back to farmhouse,
Chickens, cow,
Barnyard, fences,
Pitchfork, plow.

Family waiting,
"Where's the gold?"
Jasper shrugging,
"Warn't like told."

Dashing westward,
Forty-niners.
Jasper waving,
"Good luck, miners."